This Topsy and Tim book belongs to

_____

Topsy and Tim
At the Farm

By Jean and Gareth Adamson

Illustrations by Belinda Worsley

A catalogue record for this book is available from the British Library

Published by Ladybird Books Ltd
A Penguin Company
Penguin Books Ltd., 80 Strand, London WC2R 0RL, UK
Penguin Books Australia Ltd., 707 Collins Street, Melbourne, Victoria 3008, Australia
Penguin Group (NZ) 67 Apollo Drive, Rosedale, North Shore 0632, New Zealand

007

ISBN: 978-1-40930-336-7
Printed in China

www.topsyandtim.com

Topsy and Tim and Mummy were on their way to
Rosemary Farm. They were going to see Mummy's
friend Mrs Stewart, the farmer's wife.

"May we help on the farm?" asked Topsy.
Mrs Stewart gave them two egg-boxes.
"Go along to the hen-house," she said,
"and choose twelve nice eggs from the
hens' nests to take home."

Some hens came to greet Topsy and Tim and a duck quacked cheerfully. Topsy found some ducklings learning to swim in a little pond.

A loud hissing noise startled Topsy and Tim.
Four big, angry-looking geese were moving towards them.
"We'd better run into the hen-house," said Tim.

The hen-house felt safe, but it was very gloomy.
Soon their eyes grew used to the dark and they
could see plenty of eggs in the hens' nests.
Topsy chose six big eggs to fill her box.
Four were white and two were brown.

The angry geese were on the path back to
the farmhouse, so Topsy and Tim could
not go that way.

They climbed the wall instead, being very careful with their eggs.

"Let's go back to the farmhouse this way," said Tim.

Topsy and Tim were in the cows' meadow. They did not
know which way to turn. Then they saw Farmer Stewart.
"I'm about to take these cows to the milking sheds," said
Farmer Stewart. "Will you give me a hand?"

Topsy and Tim helped Farmer Stewart take the
cows to the milking sheds, although the cows knew
the way themselves.
"Can we help milk the cows?" asked Topsy and Tim.

"We will soon do that with our machines,
thank you," said Farmer Stewart. "I've got
a special job for you, though, if you'd care to help."

Farmer Stewart took a bucket of new milk.
He led Topsy and Tim to a smaller shed.
There was a baby calf in the shed.
"Poor thing. It wants this milk," said Farmer
Stewart, "but it can't drink. It only knows how
to suck. Put your eggs down somewhere and
then you can teach the calf how to drink from
the bucket."

Farmer Stewart showed Topsy what to do.
She dipped her finger in the milk. Then she let the
calf suck her milky finger. The calf sucked so hard
that Topsy felt nervous.

"Don't worry, it won't bite," said Farmer Stewart. Next, Topsy put her hand into the bucket. The calf went on sucking Topsy's finger until her hand and its nose were both in the warm milk. Then it was Tim's turn to feed the calf.

The calf soon discovered how to drink from the bucket without any help. Topsy and Tim ran back to the farmhouse to tell Mummy all about it.

It was time for Topsy and Tim to go home. As they walked down the lane they heard a tractor behind them. It was Farmer Stewart.

"Here are the eggs you forgot," he said, "and here is a big carton of cream for your tea, because you were so good and helpful at the farm."

*Now turn the page and help
Topsy and Tim solve a puzzle.*

Look at all these animal pictures.
Can you name the animals? Which
of these did Topsy and Tim see at
the farm today?

A Map of the Village

farm

Topsy and
Tim's house

Tony's
house

Kerry
hous

park

garage

post office

health centre

church

primary school

nursery school

police station

Have you read all the Topsy and Tim stories?

Topsy and Tim At the Farm ✓ 9781409303367	**Topsy and Tim** Go Camping ☐ 9781409303336	**Topsy and Tim** Go on an Aeroplane ☐ 9781409300571	**Topsy and Tim** Go on a Train ☐ 9781409304241	**Topsy and Tim** Go to Hospital ☐ 9781409304234
Topsy and Tim Start School ☐ 9781409300830	**Topsy and Tim** Go to the Doctor ☐ 9781409303343	**Topsy and Tim** Go to the Dentist ☐ 9781409300588	**Topsy and Tim** Have a Birthday Party ☐ 9781409300618	**Topsy and Tim** Meet Father Christmas ☐ 9781409311591
Topsy and Tim Meet the Police ☐ 9781409308836	**Topsy and Tim** Go to the Zoo ☐ 9781409300847	**Topsy and Tim** Meet the Firefighters ☐ 9781409307211	**Topsy and Tim** Learn to Swim ☐ 9781409300601	**Topsy and Tim** Play Football ☐ 9781409303350
Topsy and Tim Safety First ☐ 9781409308829	**Topsy and Tim** Sports Day ☐ 9781409309468	**Topsy and Tim** Have Itchy Heads ☐ 9781409307204	**Topsy and Tim** The New Baby ☐ 9781409300564	**Topsy and Tim** Visit London ☐ 9781409309475

Available on the App Store

The Topsy and Tim app is available for iPad, iPhone and iPod touch.

It is also available on Android devices.

Topsy and Tim

As seen on TV

Everybody's favourite twins have all sorts of experiences . . . **just like you!**

Read all about Topsy and Tim's exciting day out at the farm.

Available on the App Store

The Topsy and Tim app is available for iPad, iPhone and iPod touch.

It is also available on Android devices.

The Topsy and Tim range is available through all digital retailers.

www.topsyandtim.com

Ladybird

£4.99
CAN $9.99

ISBN 978-1-40930-336-7

Printed in China

www.ladybird.com

9 781409 303367